First American Edition 1999 by Kane/Miller Book Publishers
Brooklyn, New York & La Jolla, California

Originally published in France under the title *Idora* in 1997 by
Editions du Seuil, Paris, France

Copyright © 1997 Editions du Seuil, Paris, France
American text copyright © 1999 Kane/Miller Book Publishers

All rights reserved. For information contact:
Kane/Miller Book Publishers
P.O. Box 310529, Brooklyn, N.Y. 11231-0529

Library of Congress Cataloging-in-Publication Data

Godard, Alex.
[Idora. English]
Idora / Alex Godard ; translated by Laura McKenna. — 1st American ed.
P.   cm.
"A Cranky Nell book."
Summary: When the apartment building in which she lives is sold,
Idora, a bored and lonely giraffe, decides to make a big change in her life.
[1. Giraffes Fiction. 2. Animals Fiction. 3. Loneliness
Fiction.] I. Title.
PZ7.G53885Id   1999   [E]—dc21   99-11855

ISBN 0-916291-89-8
Printed and bound in Singapore by Tien Wah Press Pte. Ltd.
1 2 3 4 5 6 7 8 9 10

IDORA

ⴾ

ALEX GODARD

Translated by Laura McKenna

ⴾ

A CRANKY NELL BOOK

Kane/Miller Book Publishers

Brooklyn, New York & La Jolla, California

Whenever Idora felt lonely,

she would look out her apartment window

and daydream. In her mind the river would become

a wide, turquoise sea and the fog a sea spray.

The houses would become cliffs, and the sound of

Sinbad, purring as he slept on his chair, would

become the far-off pounding of waves.

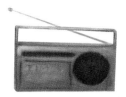

"International Day of the Giraffe!" announced

a reporter on the radio. Idora sighed. It made her

feel even lonelier. "It would be so nice if I could make

some friends," she thought. "Maybe even have a

family and perhaps during the summer take them

to the sea. I'd just like not to be alone anymore."

Ba-boom! Ba-boom! Ba-boom!

Along came Mrs. Bossanova.

The whole building danced when she walked.

"Hello, Idora! Did you read your mail yesterday?"

"No," answered Idora. She looked in her mailbox as

little as possible. She was afraid of getting bad news.

"Noooooo?" exclaimed the elephant, trying to make

herself sound important. "Well then, you don't

know the news! Our building has been sold, and we

all have to move out. They're going to tear it down."

"Move? I could never leave here," said Idora.

Worried, she went down to the river to try to calm

herself. She dreamed of where she might sail away to.

Gazing at Sinbad, she said, "All the world's a stage,

and I feel like I'm in the audience just watching.

I'm not *doing* anything."

Little by little the building emptied out.

Mr. Mole closed his gallery. Mrs. Bossanova wasn't

there to dance anymore. Nor was Miss Beethoven

in the attic playing beautiful music on her piano.

Even Elvis in the basement, who so enthusiastically

sang out "I love you!" to the twang of his

electric guitar, was gone.

Idora was utterly alone now, and like a submarine,

her spirits sank.

Spring announced itself with the roar of a bulldozer.

A huge construction crane appeared,

and soon after, a wall went up,

blocking out both the river and the sun.

Idora became terribly upset and needed to talk to

someone — anyone! Even Sinbad would do. But Sinbad

had gone out onto the landing a few

days ago to chase mice and had not returned.

Like a plant without light,

Idora felt she was withering away. What could

renew her taste for life? Nothing, absolutely nothing.

 Unless. . . . Could she? Did she dare?

All of a sudden Idora got up and left the house.

As she walked along the river,

everything — the whole world! — seemed as if

it was spinning around her. But it didn't matter.

She had a plan.

Idora did not stop.

No more daydreaming for her.

"I'd like a one-way ticket south, please!"

she said as she stepped up to the

window at the railway station.

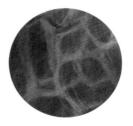

Eyes closed, Idora let the rhythm

of the train rock her to sleep.

She no longer felt so lonely.

For so long, Idora had yearned to live

a life full of adventure, and now she would.

There was no reason to be sad anymore.

The sun was rising on the first day of her new life.

She was on an express train to the sea

she had only dreamt of!

Outside, thick woods of yellow trees

brightened the sky like bouquets of light.

The air smelled of lavender and pine. . . .

The world was full of hope. . . . Idora took a deep breath.

She felt very excited and very happy.